W9-BTO-431

EARLY BIRD
STORIES

Snarky Sharky

Early★Reader

First American edition published in 2023 by Lerner Publishing Group, Inc.

An original concept by Lou Treleaven
Copyright © 2023 Lou Treleaven

Illustrated by Angelika Scudamore

First published by Maverick Arts Publishing Limited

Maverick
arts publishing

Licensed Edition
Snarky Sharky

Lerner Publications Company
An imprint of Lerner Publishing Group, Inc.
241 First Avenue North
Minneapolis, MN 55401 USA

For reading levels and more information, look up this title at www.lernerbooks.com.

Main body text set in Mikado a. Typeface provided by HVD Fonts.

Library of Congress Cataloging-in-Publication Data

Names: Treleaven, Lou, author. | Scudamore, Angelika, illustrator.
Title: Snarky Sharky / Lou Treleaven ; illustrated by Angelika Scudamore.
Description: First American edition. | Minneapolis : Lerner Publications, 2023. | Series: Early bird readers. Green (Early bird stories) | "First published by Maverick Arts Publishing Limited"—Page facing title page. | Audience: Ages 8–9. | Audience: Grades K–1. | Summary: "Snarky Sharky is snappy and grumpy. Luckily, Snarky's friends keep trying to brighten her day. This story about a shark and her dreaded mornings introduces young children to reading"— Provided by publisher.
Identifiers: LCCN 2021055138 (print) | LCCN 2021055139 (ebook) | ISBN 9781728438504 (lib. bdg.) | ISBN 9781728448381 (pbk.) | ISBN 9781728444611 (eb pdf)
Subjects: LCSH: Readers (Primary) | LCGFT: Readers (Publications)
Classification: LCC PE1119.2 .T7478 2023 (print) | LCC PE1119.2 (ebook) | DDC 428.6/2—dc23/eng/20211130

LC record available at https://lccn.loc.gov/2021055138
LC ebook record available at https://lccn.loc.gov/2021055139

Manufactured in the United States of America
1-49673-49593-12/6/2021

EARLY BIRD
STORIES

Snarky Sharky

Lou Treleaven   illustrated by
Angelika Scudamore

Lerner Publications ◆ Minneapolis

Snarky Sharky was very snarky.

She was grumpy. She was snappy.

Everyone was scared of Snarky Sharky, even her friends.

"Good morning, Snarky Sharky," said Friendly Flatfish.

"What's good about it? Nothing!
Go away," said Snarky Sharky.

"Good morning, Snarky Sharky,"
said Jolly Jellyfish.

"It's not a good morning, it's a bad morning!" said Snarky Sharky. "Goodbye!"

"Good morning, Snarky Sharky," said Cool Clam. "Chill out, dude."

"And you can shut your shell too," said Snarky Sharky.

Her friends tried everything they could to cheer Snarky Sharky up.

They hung seaweed around her cave.

They changed the bulb in her anglerfish.

They even polished her spare rows of teeth. At least, they tried.

That evening, Snarky Sharky
seemed a bit happier.
Her friends crossed their fins.

But in the morning, Snarky Sharky
was as Snarky as ever.

Snarky Sharky's friends had a
secret meeting.

"She's only really scary in the
mornings," said Friendly Flatfish.

"Maybe she just hates mornings?"
said Jolly Jellyfish.

"You could be right, man,"
said Cool Clam.

The next morning,

everyone was very quiet.

Friendly Flatfish swam

around extra slowly.

Cool Clam closed his shell
extra quietly.

Jolly Jellyfish stung people
extra softly.

And Snarky Sharky slept in!

When she finally came out of her cave, Snarky Sharky felt much better.

And her friends never had to say, "good morning, Snarky Sharky," ever again.

They said, "good afternoon, Sharky," instead!

Quiz

1. What is one of the things Snarky Sharky's friends did to cheer her up?
   a) Changed the bulb in her anglerfish
   b) Threw her a party
   c) Made her a cake

2. When is Snarky Sharky mostly scary?
   a) Mornings
   b) Afternoons
   c) Evenings

3. What did the friends do to help?
   a) They made lots of noise
   b) They gave her gifts
   c) They were very quiet

4. Snarky Sharky . . .

    a) Took a bath

    b) Slept in

    c) Took a vacation

5. What do the friends now say to Snarky Sharky when she gets up?

    a) Hello, Snarky Sharky

    b) Good afternoon, Sharky

    c) Good evening, Shark

Leveled for Guided Reading

Early Bird Stories have been edited and leveled by leading educational consultants to correspond with guided reading levels. The levels are assigned by taking into account the content, language style, layout, and phonics used in each book. Visit www.lernerbooks.com for more Early Bird Readers titles!

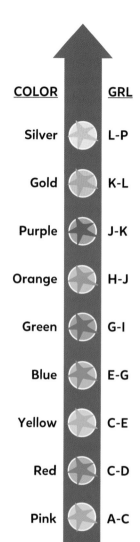

COLOR	GRL
Silver	L-P
Gold	K-L
Purple	J-K
Orange	H-J
Green	G-I
Blue	E-G
Yellow	C-E
Red	C-D
Pink	A-C